ASTILLA

J L CAREY JR

BLACK MADONNA PRESS
P.O. Box 183
Otter Lake, MI
48464-0183

Book design by Broken Cog Media:

Copyright © 2018 by J L Carey Jr

ISBN: 978-1-387-55734-9

A special thanks to Yahoo for first publishing the story in its raw form in 2010. Also, to Alan Kaekel for further editing, revision and inspiration.

All Rights Reserved. No part of this book may be used or reproduced in any manner without written permission except in the case of brief quotations embodied in critical articles and reviews.

For Jackson Mathew Carey

Chapter One

It was a clear cool October night, the kind of night that makes your eyes water when you stare into space. Charlie sat out on the front porch smoking a cigarette with Brian. They always sat outside while Charlie smoked.

Charlie had the idea that if he smoked outside eventually he would quit. After two years though, it just became habit to smoke out on the front porch. He had tried the vaping thing too and though it was fun it just wasn't the same.

Brian found smoking to be a disgusting habit and would tell Charlie so, as he spit his chew into an empty Pepsi bottle. There was always a dip in his lower lip and there was always a friendly razzing. At any rate, Brian enjoyed sitting on the front porch and as he made another deposit into his 20 oz plastic spittoon, he spit then pushed at Charlie with his foot to try and knock him over. Charlie had taken the last drag off his cigarette, leaned over towards the front door and dragged the plastic Folgers butt-kit closer to him. His face turned red as he leaned over the arm of the lawn chair, mashed his cigarette out and tried to keep from falling out.

"Cut it out you dick," Charlie giggled.

"You're never going to quit," Brian jabbed reclining in his chair until his eyes caught several bursts of light speckle in the starlit sky. Some of the bursts streaked along and then fizzled out, but one seemed to burn brighter and brighter. "Holy crap dude do you see this?" Brian yelled as Charlie made his final press to ensure the smoke had gone out.

When Charlie looked up, Brian fell out of his chair, spilling the contents of his Pepsi bottle. Charlie just watched in awe as what seemed like a small piece of the sun went roaring past the front porch. The projectile blazed, tearing a hole through the elm that stood in the side yard and then went on to obliterate the neighbor's barn.

Dumbfounded, Charlie stood up and gaped at the tree that was burning like Liberties torch in the night. Embers trailed off into the dark sky as the wind rustled them loose then carried them away. "Holy shit," Charlie said. "That bitch is burning like the Queen of Babylon."

Brian managed to right himself, muttering his disbelief that they were still alive.

Next door at the Bernalillo's, it was a typical Thursday night. Maria was lying in bed reading the latest romance novel from her book club. Her husband Fernando, on the other hand, was tinkering on the Internet. With a click, he signed off from some questionably acceptable romance material of his own. Rubbing his eyes and yawning, he made his way to the kitchen to get a drink of water. Two gulps in, Fernando choked as the meteor suddenly incinerated his barn. The explosion sent a shock wave through the home as the dishes on the counter rattled.

With horror, Fernando opened the back door and ran outside. He had expected to find that a plane had crashed in his backyard. To his dismay, all that was there was a smoldering crater where his barn used to sit.

"Holy, Jesus," he let out in confusion.

"Nando! What's happened honey?" Maria yelled with panic as she ran up behind her husband.

"Something hit the barn."

Back around the crater, the flickers of fire twinkled in the yard like a scattering of stars. They hissed and popped as the coals smoldered around the cone shaped meteorite in the center of the crater. For a moment the meteor lie nestled snug in the scorched earth. As it cooled though, it began to open, like a hideous pinecone chard in a forest fire. Its needles stretched out in the thousands and with a sudden poof were dispersed throughout the lawn. It was as if an enormous porcupine had spread out and then spontaneously combusted.

The sound of fire engines cried in the distance. Fernando and Maria edged their way back, curious to see the impact site. As they got closer two heads popped up over the top of the fence.

"Are you guys okay?" Brian asked while looking at the hole in the ground.

"Yes. Nothing happened to the house luckily," Fernando said. "What the heck was that?"

Charlie laughed, "It was a meteor."

"Yeah," Brian added. "I saw a bunch of falling stars for a second, but this one just kept coming." With a slight tilt of his head he spit his chew onto the ground. "Don't worry though. I made a wish on it."

As the four of them chortled Fernando rubbed his scalp, let out a sigh then he and Maria walked closer to the craters edge. Fernando took another step forward, letting out a shriek of pain. Still giggling, the others did not understand what was happening. Maria's eyes grew frantic as she stopped laughing and asked him repeatedly what was wrong.

Bewildered by the man's sudden reaction, Brian and Charlie prepared to jump the fence when they heard two fire trucks, a police car and a paramedic roll up to the house. Charlie hopped off the brace of the fence and ran over to the team of fire fighters. The air seemed to fill with the hum of engines and the smell of diesel fuel. Some of the firefighters began reeling a hose towards the burning tree.

"There's something wrong with my neighbor," Charlie shouted. "He's just over the fence."

Two of the firefighters approached him. One of them, fireman Casey, asked Charlie what he had said as the other looked out towards the fence and noticed Brian, still perched on it and signaling for them to come quick.

"I said there's something wrong with my neighbor," Charlie repeated, pointing out to the fence.

Casey signaled at the paramedic, who had just slipped his cell phone into his pocket. The man nodded and started over towards them, passing the other firefighters as they began spraying water on what was left of the elm tree.

As the paramedic got closer, some of the other firemen began running back towards the fence also. When they reached it, Casey's partner struck the two support beams with his axe, popping them loose from the pole. The other men then pushed on the fencing until it fell over.

The team of responders was surprised to find the giant crater on the other side. They quickly made their way around it to Fernando, who was sitting on the ground with one slipper off and holding his foot. With intense pain in his face, Fernando rocked back and forth.

"What seems to be the issue?" the paramedic urged.

Maria tried to explain to Greg, the paramedic, that Nando had stepped on a splinter and that she thought it was from the barn. "I tried to pull it out of my husband's foot, but the astilla seemed to melt and then was gone."

Greg knelt down and looked at Fernando's foot. "As far as I can tell, there is no injury," he said as he ran his index finger down the center of Fernando's foot causing him to flinch.

"So you can feel that alright?" Greg questioned Fernando with a smile. "Does it hurt when I press on it?" he asked as he pushed with his thumb.

"No," he answered. "Actually, it is starting to feel a little better."

"If you would like I could take you to the hospital to have it looked at further? Who knows what you really stepped on; could have been an old piece of the barn," he puzzled, "or it could be something else." With a sigh he rested Fernando's foot on the ground. "Whatever it was it still could've been hot from the looks of that crater."

"Looks like you had a bomb go off in your backyard to me," Casey added.

"Do you want to go to the hospital honey," Maria asked as she rubbed her husband's back.

"No. I think I will be okay. I'm not going to the hospital over some stupid little astilla."

"But what if there is still a piece of the splinter in your foot? What if you get the tetanus?"

Fernando rubbed his head and huffed. "If it is still bothering me tomorrow than I will go see the doctor." With that, he pressed his hands on the ground and tried to stand up. Greg and Casey proceeded to grab him by both arms and help him to his good foot.

"You alright?" Charlie asked.

"Yes," he said wobbly. "I'm fine. It was just a splinter."

"Why don't you let us help you into the house?" Greg offered.

"I can manage. Thank you," Fernando said with some annoyance. "Thank you for destroying my fence also. It's not like I didn't have enough property damage already tonight."

"We were just trying to help," said Casey, with some confusion in his voice.

"Well you can help me by leaving my property," grumbled Fernando as he hobbled his way back towards the house. "I'll call the insurance company tomorrow and see if they cover an 'act of god' or whatever the hell else you want to call it."

"I apologize," implored Maria. "This has been very stressful on my husband. He loved that old barn and I know he feels extremely embarrassed over the splinter."

"That's all right ma'am," Greg said. "That kind of stuff happens all the time. It's going to be awhile though before all the people clear off your property. In fact, here comes the press and what looks like some scientists of some sort."

Maria looked through the break in the fence to see a large group of people heading towards them. Along with the media there were meteor hunters eager to find a piece of the alien rock and what looked like government agents in hazmat suits, some waving Geiger counters and others carrying gear marked FEMA. "Well. I am going to go and make sure my husband is alright. Thank you all for your help. If there is anything you need, just let me know."

"All right ma'am," Greg responded.

Brian and Charlie waved to her as she walked away. "We'll see you later Maria," Charlie added.

"Goodnight boys," Maria replied with a faint smile. The smile did nothing really to disguise the tired and stressed look on her face. It was obvious she had been a bit embarrassed herself and wanted no part of talking to the press.

Brian scooped the chew from his mouth with his index finger as he watched Maria walk back to the house. He waited until he felt she was out of earshot and then he mentioned how strange it was about Fernando's reaction to the splinter. The other men agreed with him and Casey even called him a Nancy boy for being such a sissy about the whole thing. They all laughed about the wise crack, until one of the reporters on sight fell to the ground with a horrible shriek of pain.

Chapter Two

Once inside their home, things seemed to calm down for the Bernalillo's as much as it could be expected with the circus forming in their backyard. Still limping, Fernando assured his wife that everything was fine and that he had simply over reacted. Kissing Maria on the forehead, he untied the belt of her robe and slipped the garment off her shoulders. The robe fell to the floor as she melted into her husband's arms, the smooth silk of her pajamas pressed against him. He held her tight with his arms wrapped around her. She did the same and as she held him, Maria slid her hand into the back of his t-shirt.

"Ooh! Nando. Your skin is freezing cold," she said, pulling slightly away from him.

Fernando smiled. "Yes. So don't move away from me. I need you to keep me warm."

She smiled at him as well and ordered him under the covers of the bed. Without argument, he kissed her again and slid under the covers. Maria went to the window, looked at the frenzy of people a last time then released the roman shade over the window. Then, switching off the light, followed her husband into bed and pressed her body against him.

The cold of his body made all the hair of her body stand on end. Still, Maria's exhaustion far outweighed the torment of her husband's frigid skin. Within a matter of minutes the couple had passed out.

Shortly after dosing, Fernando became restless and awoke. Maria lay quietly as he sat up shivering. For him, it was as if he had awakened in an icebox. As his teeth chattered, Fernando rubbed his skin with his hands in a futile attempt to warm himself. He stared at what seemed like millions of goose bumps covering his body.

Panicked, he got out of bed and stumbled to the bathroom. When he turned on the light he was mortified to find that his skin was a grayish blue. A crawl went down his spine causing him to shiver convulsively as he tore the shower curtain open, ripping it from three of its rings.

Teeth chattering convulsively, Fernando turned the hot water on and began filling the tub. It was all he could think of at the moment. He had to get warm. Clawing at his cloths, he flung them off and climbed into the steaming bath. His mind began to race in confusion as he sat in the scalding tub, his body still shaking. The terrible grayish blue became a dark smoke gray as his eyes rolled back into his head, as his jaw locked open, as the muscles of his body constricted.

When Maria awoke she sat strait up and gasped. She did not understand what had woken her and for the moment it seemed an unmemorable nightmare or as though something unspeakable had been standing over her and watching her sleep. Her hands felt for a security, which was not there. This only increased the anxiety she was feeling and as she tried to catch her breath, she heard the sound of water running.

"Nando," she cried out, but there was no response only the darkness of the room and faint light that gleaned from beneath the bathroom door. This gave her an uneasy feeling in her stomach. "Nando," she said again as she climbed out of bed, letting out a sigh of disgust as her foot hit the sopping wet carpet. The water squishing between her toes as she made her way to the bathroom.

Part of her did not want to open the door for she feared what she would find, something stronger compelled her though as she bit her bottom lip and turned the doorknob. When she pulled the door open, visions of her seeing her dead husband in the tub mortified her. Peeking around the corner Maria found the tub poring over with water, but no Fernando. She was happily relieved and at the same time furious for what she believed now to be her husband's carelessness that caused this.

Shaking her head, she stomped into the bathroom, splashing on the linoleum floor. There was a strange smell that seemed to linger. It caught Maria's attention for a second as she reached over the tub and shut the water off. It was when she did this that she noticed a dark gray blob at the bottom of the tub. As her brain entered a state of denial and rationalization she slipped her hand into the water to retrieve what could only be, she thought, a sopping wet blanket. The reality came though as she stood up and unfolded the dripping skin of her husband; the remnant form of his body captured in a snake like molting.

Maria screamed, as the world seemed to close in around her. She ran from the bathroom, slipping slightly on the wet floor. The tears flooded her eyes as she made her way down the dark hall and into the kitchen.

Franticly, she flicked the small light on over the counter and grabbed her cell phone. As she dialed 911 her eye caught a shadow in the living room. It moved only slightly, but enough to notice the change on the floor.

Again that strange sweet smell permeated her nostrils. A smell like nothing she had ever known and so overpowering that it dizzied her.

"Nando?" Maria uttered weeping as she moved to the opening between the kitchen and the living room.

The 911 operator answered and began asking if there was an emergency? Maria could not respond. Her eyes blinked rapidly and welted up with even more tears.

Before her, crouched along the far wall of the living room was a gray spiked creature. It turned its long head towards her, exposing its grizzly teeth. Its eyes were large and black and cradled in its long razor claws was a human head.

In shock, Maria became incoherent. She started to weep in both Spanish and English, causing the 911 operator to become distressed as well. Maria wanted to scream, but the terror of what she was seeing combined with her sobbing kept her breathless and frozen.

The creature growled with a low rattle, then turned its attention away from Maria, dropping the severed head it was holding to the hardwood floor. The head wobbled and rolled for a moment, coming to rest on the rug with its awful eyes fixed in her direction.

This was more than Maria could handle. Nearly fainting, she fell to the floor and began to vomit, for the eyes that gazed at her so frightfully were those of fireman Casey.

The 911 operator was pleading with her to respond and began telling her that assistance was on the way, that she should try to stay calm, but in shock began to rock back and forth, falling into a dream. Her fragile psyche broke. With her head now buried in her knees, she rocked and mumbled.

The creature, no longer concerned with her, returned to its meal. In the corner of the living room was the disemboweled carcass of fireman Casey. His uniform was shredded and now only small identifiable remnants remained clinging to his lacerated flesh. One of his boots still hugged his foot as if it were in denial of its wearer's demise.

With its back flared, the killer snorted as it drove its snout into the dismal feast. Its long blade like claws cut away at the downed prey. The razor teeth tore at the sinews as it greedily swallowed, hardly taking a moment to breathe. Like a pig in a feeding frenzy, it gorged cracking through the bones as it went.

The dim light from the front porch shone through the window of the living room. The murky shadow of the monster danced on the blood-spattered floor. Its long gray quills stood upright from its back and spine, pulsing as it devoured, adding to the horror of the shadow.

Maria mumbled low, inaudible.

Suddenly, the creature was roused. Its head batted in the air for a moment as its mouth hissed, teeth gleamed and blood came drooling from the corners. It turned its head back and peered its eyes out the window. Then it was gone, gone into the early morning darkness, disappearing through the open front door.

Maria was still rocking when the first two police officers walked into her home. Their flashlights eyed the mutilation. One of the officers nearly fainted. The other officer recognized Maria from earlier that evening. It was State Trooper Adam Douglas.

When Adam and his partner were approaching the house he got a terrible uneasiness. From the drive they could see the front door open. It wasn't until they walked up closer and noticed the smear of blood that stretched from the sidewalk into the house that his nerves began to frazzle. When his partner Jon Littleton half fainted though, it felt as if something had snapped in his brain. His mind twisted as he moved past the carnage to the suffering woman on the kitchen floor.

Adam then looked over at Jon who was trying to compose himself. The young trooper took a knee and pressed his shoulder against the wall just inside the door. He had vomited down the front of his dark blue uniform and as he breathed in heavily his eyes looked franticly about the dark house for the thing that could have done this.

Seeing that Jon was going to be all right, Adam began looking all over. It had occurred to him also that whatever had taken this fireman's life may still be there in the house. When he knelt down to Maria he did not notice her mumble, he just tried to calm her rocking. Unsuccessful, he reached for the button of his radio to call for backup. Adam's hands shook as he pressed, the corner of his eye glimpsing first the boot then fixing on the face that stared its hollow look from the rug, that terribly recognizable artifact, an image that would haunt him to the end.

His voice resonated in the room, "Yeah. God, I need…" he said, with his stomach beginning to force its way into his throat. "I need some back up here right now. We've got a serious situation."

Chapter Three

When the other officers arrived on the scene, what should have been quietly contained became a media frenzy. Around a dozen State and local squad cars came barreling up to the Bernalillo's home. This drew the attention of the two dozen photographers and press agents who were in the backyard still working on the meteor story. Many of them chattered as they walked to the house about how this could have happened right under their noses? All of them confessed to hearing nothing and that they had not realized that Fireman Casey had even gone missing.

Fire fighters concerned about Casey also arrived soon after as the word spread that something awful had taken place at the Bernalillo's. Neighbors from all the surrounding homes came out and some of the scientists had come to find out what all the fuss was about.

Some men from the government arrived when the paramedics wheeled Maria out. Photographers shamefully snapped away at Maria's tormented and sedated face. As the EMS team placed her into the ambulance, one of the Government agents asked Greg if she had seen what had happened then gestured for two FEMA members to escort her inside the ambulance.

Greg shrugged, and told the man that all she keeps saying is "El Chupacabra. El Chupacabra."

He then climbed into the back of the ambulance and swung the door half shut. "She's in shock right now. She's not going to make any sense." With that, Greg closed the door on the man and the ambulance drove away.

One of the reporters then asked the agent "What the hell is El Chupacabra?" but the agent, ignoring him, turned away.

Minutes after Maria left Troopers Adam and Jon came out of the home. They were instantly greeted by a mob from the press. The reporter who questioned the agent scrambled up to the rabble while scribbling something in his note pad.

The press shouted at the two officers, demanding to know what was happening. Before they could answer though, the officers were hurried away by the government agents. As the agent's vehicles sped off, Pave Hawk helicopters flew in over the site. The sky seemed pocked with choppers as they combed the area from above.

A FEMA team also arrived. One group started herding the mass of people away from the house while the other group set up a quarantine area around the perimeter of the yard. Even the officers investigating the case were sealed from the area and taken for testing.

During the excitement Brian and Charlie had come out of their home. As they walked down the street towards the Bernalillo's house the white FEMA trucks zipped past them. When they arrived at the house they were met in the street by one of their neighbors Mark. Mark was standing in front of the house, his hand resting on the yellow tape that had created a barrier into the Bernalillo's yard. He was wearing sandals, boxer shorts, a University of Michigan sweatshirt and a snowcap. This was usually how they found him.

Beside Mark was his girlfriend Kay who still looked half-asleep in her sock feet and long thick terrycloth robe. She yawned taking her eyes from the Pave Hawks above as Brian and Charlie walked up to them.

"Oh yeah?" Charlie said as he greeted his friends.

"You missed it," Mark began. "They wheeled Maria out of here on a stretcher. I think Fernando got killed or something."

"Really?" Brian replied, looking up towards the house. "That's messed up."

"Yeah. Kay and I heard one of the officers say that they think it could be a serial killer."

"Great!" Charlie responded. "That's just what we need," he muttered, shaking his head with disbelief.

"I know," Kay agreed, "I won't be able to flipping sleep now with some wacko running around." As she said this, a man in a white hazmat suit motioned for them to move back away from the yellow tape.

The cold morning air made Charlie's nose start to run. He sniffled as he stepped back and watched the FEMA team go in and out of the house. They all looked as if they were in a terrible hurry and on one of their trips he noticed that two of them were carrying a stretcher. On the stretcher was a black body bag and behind them came a third person carrying a smaller black bag. They loaded the surreal cargo into their white truck and the driver rushed it away.

The group just stood in silence as they watched it drive into the distance. Brian pulled his can of chew out of his pocket and started smacking it on his fingers. Charlie took out his cigarettes, pulled one out of the box and placed it in his mouth. Mark and Kay then signaled for Charlie to give them one as well.

No one could believe what was happening. Before last night nothing big had ever really happened in Lapeer. It was a fairly small town and aside from having a prizewinning horse farm, it had never been mentioned in the national news. Now they were the focus of attention all over the globe.

Across the street from the Bernalillo's home, below the whirr of helicopters in the cold clear sky and just a few rows into the tall weathered corn, a pair of eyes watched anxiously. The eyes were poised low and peered through the heavy breath that clung to the icy morning air.

There was a thirst in the breathing as Brian and Charlie said their goodbyes to Mark and Kay, the crouching predator stirring. Not knowing they were being stalked, the two friends turned and started home. For the creature, the hunt had begun.

The Chupacabra picked up pace in the corn, rustling the dry stalks as it went. Oblivious to their danger, Charlie pitched the butt of his smoke as they rounded the corner to their street.

Brian was about to say something to Charlie when the Chupacabra leapt from the field. When its long nine-inch talon like claws struck the pavement they made a hideous clack. The sound caught the two's attention, causing them to whirl around.

As the Chupacabra made another leap closer, a UPS truck suddenly struck it. The creature came out so fast the driver did not see it until it was bouncing off his grill. The force of the big ugly brown truck sent the creature rolling for nearly twenty feet.

Everyone had thought the driver had struck a dog. Mark and Kay, who were walking onto their front porch, had not taken notice of it until they heard the thud. After the thing stopped rolling and came to a rest, Kay, thinking it was a dog, ran out to it.

The Chupacabra's chest heaved as it lay unconscious in the middle of the road. Kay ran up to it, not really looking at what it was and when she turned to tell Mark to call animal control it awoke.

As her head faced forward Mark screamed out, but the claws split her from her left shoulder to her right thigh. Her intestines spilling out as the creature's jaws snapped around her neck.

Before Mark could even reach the street, the Chupacabra had disappeared with Kay into the corn. Brian and Charlie reached Mark just in time to stop him from chasing them into the field. Mark's sweatshirt tore as the two held him back. His face filled with tears of panic and rage as he swung wildly to break free. One of his swings struck Charlie in the face, turning it instantly red.

Dazed, Charlie righted himself, still holding onto Mark. His fingers twisted in the disheveled sweat-shirt. Brian managed to get in front of him, clamping his arms around Marks chest and pressing him back.

"Let me go," Mark shouted.

Brian just stood firm. "No. You're not going in there."

"Just let me go. I have to get her," Mark let out with a heart full of pain. He made a final attempt to throw himself loose. "Let me.... Go."

"Mark. You're not going into the field," Charlie screamed. "That thing will kill you too."

All of Marks' energy depleted. The two friends held him as the FEMA team moved past them. They had peeled off their white protective suits and beneath were wearing Military uniforms. Some of them wore gas masks and carried automatic weapons. Others wore masks and carried flame-throwers. The group of friends looked on angrily as it was apparent now that these soldiers and FEMA agents were prepared for something they were not telling the public.

More troops ascended as the Pave Hawk helicopters landed in the road. From one of the choppers came a man that signaled to the assembling team while talking on a radio. More helicopters flew over and within ten minutes several military vehicles arrived. The three friends were then placed in a jeep and taken to what they were told would be a safer area, while the soldiers with flame-throwers lit their weapons.

One of the soldiers stopped the man with the radio and asked him, "How do you like yours, sir?"

Placing a half-smoked cigar into his mouth and lighting it he replied, "Extra crispy private; extra crispy."

With that, the flame-throwers moved in, sweeping along the base of the dry weathered corn and igniting the first few rows. The smell of smoke and popcorn rose into the air. It caused the Chupacabra to pause for a moment, the corn rustling in the breeze as it lifted its snout into the air, snorted then clutched its prey again.

The Army had set up a perimeter around the entire field. The idea was to contain it, move in on it from all sides and then destroy it. Most of the soldiers did not know what they were attempting to kill they were simply given an order. For the few who did know, their plan was working perfectly, in fact too perfect, but they had severely underestimated their enemy.

To the Colonel directing operations it seemed the world was on fire. He stood at the edge of the field and watched as the smoke plumed into the air, suffocating the sun. When the troops reached the center he received a call on his radio. They had surrounded the Chupacabra.

Chewing on the wet end of this cigar, he lit the stogy again and took a final puff then pitched it into the street. The colonel made his way to the center, as his boots trod over the ashes and charred corn as he went. The smoke loomed in the air as he went and when he reached his men he stood before them looking at the creature.

The men whispered with confusion. They wondered what it was they had found and how it managed to drag the woman it had beside it. Many of them were anxious just to kill it.

The Chupacabra had curled into a ball. Its needles in the thousands stood on end. As it stayed there, its skin seemed to turn to stone, an almost shale like appearance.

The Colonel, recognizing the young private, waved him over. "Well son. You promised me extra crispy. Destroy that overgrown porcupine son of a bitch."

"Yes, sir," the private sounded off, turning his flame-thrower on the creature. The ball of needles lit up receiving the flames while several other soldiers blazed away at it also.

The needles popped and crackled, sometimes hissing while that strange smell drifted through the filters of their masks; that smell, like honey, but somehow different, lulling and terrible.

17

When the flame-throwers finally stopped the Chupacabra sat sizzling and smoldering in the dirt. Then, without warning, it suddenly exploded. The screams of agony from the soldiers were nearly simultaneous as thousands of long sliver like quills were hurled into them. Not a soldier was left standing once the rain of needles ended. In this smoldering field of wails and astilla's, the DNA strands were planted.

Chapter Four

Fifteen minutes away from the scene, the old Imlay City fairgrounds had been converted into a FEMA camp. Military vehicles sat in ready, as did the national news vans. When Brian, Charlie and Mark rolled in, it was obvious that this was something much greater than a serial killer or rabid wild dog.

They were greeted at the medical station by a group of men in biological suits who rushed them into the tent. Each of the friends was then stripped and given a contamination shower. The shower consisted of two medics scrubbing each contaminated person down in extremely hot water. The contaminated individual is then scoured over their entire body with a wire brush until a layer of skin is removed.

Once the showers were completed, a series of blood tests and shots were administered, but never really explained. It wasn't until they found themselves in a room with Officer Adam Douglas that some truths began to surface.

The friends were glad to see a familiar face in the room as they sat down next to him. The three men grimaced with pain as they eased into the metal folding chairs. Brian sat with his body cocked to one side. "I'm surprised they didn't stick that wire brush up my ass and scrub my colon," he said while attempting to keep as much weight off his rear as possible without actually standing up again. The others, except for Mark, laughed and winced at the same time. Mark just sat with his hands over his eyes until his breakdown became apparent to everyone.

"Shit," Charlie said as he leaned towards Mark and put his arm around him. "I'm so sorry about Kay brother."

"I just can't believe it," Mark mumbled. "It just can't be real." The tears streamed down his face as he spoke. "It can't be real."

"We're going to figure this out," Brian said. "Plus our troops are going to kill that fucking thing."

After several minutes of sitting in discomfort, a woman dressed in a stark black suit entered the tent. She walked at an easy pace, coming to a stop around ten feet in front of the semi-attentive men.

Adam was the first to speak. "So are you going to tell us what the hell we are doing here? Oh, and while you're at it, maybe you could explain why two goons threw me into a boiling shower and then proceeded to sand parts of my body that I didn't realize I had?"

The woman, who appeared to be in her mid thirties, walked a few steps closer to Adam. She looked at him with distress in her warm brown eyes and clenching jaw. Dropping her head for a moment, she broke eye contact, looked up at the other men briefly and then reestablished her train of vision towards Adam.

"I know y'all are wondering what is going on. I'm going to try and brief you as clear as possible. Some of you, I understand, have seen some things that have maybe raised some questions in y'alls minds…"

"Yeah! What in God's name killed my girlfriend?" Mark shouted, as he stood up from his chair. His eyes were puffed and red and he was clearly still ready to burst into tears again.

A rending pain welled in the woman's wide eyes. "Look. I am very sorry for your loss, but you're not the only one who's lost a love one. I know y'all must have seen the soldiers who went after that monster. My brother was one of the soldiers that went into that field and none of them came out alive."

Everyone was silent for a moment. Mark just stood there looking as if he had swallowed his tongue.

"Again, I'm sorry, sir. I know how difficult this must be for you," she said, wiping her eyes with the palms of her hands. "Also, I want to apologize to everyone for those grueling showers. They were necessary though. You and everyone here cannot risk contamination from that being."

"Umm – Excuse me. We didn't get your name," Adam said with a smile, breaking some of the tension in the room. "My name is Adam Douglas."

"Oh – Yes – I'm sorry. You're Officer Adam Douglas, correct?"

Adam, still smiling, nodded his head yes.

Wiping her eye a last time, she forced a smile. "My name is special agent Anna May Tidwell. I'm part of a special task force that hunts and destroys certain types of anomalies. In this case it appears that we are after a Gene Stealer or more commonly referred to as an el Chupacabra."

"A what?" Adam asked, his smile melting off his face.

"A Chupacabra," she restated. "It means goat sucker, but they obviously do not hunt goats exclusively, especially this aberrant variety that you encountered earlier today."

"Does this have anything to do with the meteor that crashed into my neighbor's yard last night?" Charlie said, while raising his hand up.

"Are you Charlie Lockwood?" Anna Asked.

"Yeah."

"Yes, Charlie. Well, we are investigating that possibility right now and there is a very good likelihood that the two events are not coincidental."

Brian stood up now, scratching his raw arm. "So are you saying that that thing is from space?"

"I'm saying that it could be."

"And what did you call it? A Chu-paaa-cobra? Is that the word for giant alien space dog or something?"

Charlie giggled a little causing the others to smile some as well. Brian, still standing, started scratching his back now. Anna approached him, turned him about face and rubbed his back with the palm of her hand.

"The showers y'all were given will have much the same effect as a sun burn, so it's best not to scratch with your fingernails. As for giant alien space dogs, that's to be decided," she said smiling.

With a light pat on the back Anna stepped away from Brian. Brian, smiling, eased back into his chair and shot Charlie a boasting look.

"The Chupacabra," she began again, "actually got its name from the Puerto Rican's. One of these creatures was first sited there in March of 1995. It had slaughtered an entire field of goats. Upon investigating this anomaly though I found that similar creatures have been cited for quite some time. In 1872 Lewis Carroll refers to this creature in a poem titled *Jabberwocky*. Carroll wrote, 'Beware the Jabberwock, my son! / The jaws that bite, the claws that catch! / Beware the Jubjub bird, and shun / The frumious Bandersnatch!' The Russian version of this creature is what concerns us though."

Adam ran his hands through his hair and exhaled. "So you're saying that these things drop out of space every so often, go on a killing spree and then just seem to disappear?"

"In the past this was the case, but recently it's changed," Anna paused for a moment. "We believe the Chupacabra has – evolved."

With a startling shriek a siren began bellowing through the camp. The sound was nearly deafening and unraveled the men's nerves. Adam went to Anna and grabbed her shoulder.

"What's happening?"

Anna looked him in the face. "Something very bad is happening," she yelled as the siren drummed out her voice. "Y'all have to stay here. I need you to stay safe inside. This alarm means we're under attack."

"Where is my partner, Jon?"

"He's safe. He's in quarantine, Adam. I'll finish my briefing when I get back. Stay inside," she yelled as she ran to the door. The siren screamed as she opened the door to the tent and then she was gone.

The four men stood in the room listening to the mayhem outside between the glaring shrieks that permeated the air. They could hear the sounds of the trucks running mingled with the smell of fuel. There were scattered voices, all of them urgent and panicked. Shadows moved along the outer wall of the tent as Charlie moved to the corner of the room. There on the table was a laptop. Opening it up, Charlie turned it on the small folding table that stood in front of the chairs so they could all see the screen. Making sure it was plugged in he pressed the power button and turned it on. The rest of the guys grew attentive as the screen lit up.

It took a moment for Charlie to find the live stream of the news, but to their surprise they saw the outside of their compound at the fairgrounds. The Channel Five News crew was reporting the action-live. Troops scurried through local town's people who had been evacuated to the FEMA camp. There was a look of terror on the people's faces as they pooled together. Tanks and armored vehicles moved slowly through the herds of innocents.

The camera then moved wildly, unable to stay focused on the announcing reporter as screams rang out with the sudden explosion of gunfire. Blood curdling cries flooded the air as the Chupacabra's cut through the ranks.

Several of the creatures moved as though they were weightless shadows. Their tyrannical claws were non-distinctive, cutting down anything within their grasp. It was as if a horde of alien velociraptors had come to devour the world. Despite the torrent of gunfire many soldiers were unable to hit the creatures unless they stopped to feed. The rounds did not always stop them. Some of the Chupacabra's that were hit were only enraged, leaping onto the vehicle and devouring the gunman. The few Chupacabra's that died curled into balls as the life left them, splaying the needles upon their backs.

Occasionally, shadows of the creatures waved along the outer wall of the tent. The four men inside rummaged through the pile of equipment in the corner looking for any type of weapon in which to defend themselves. This proved to be fruitless and extremely despairing.

"There's not even a freakin' Buck knife in here!" Mark bellowed as he heaved another box of medical supplies aside. Brian just stood in silence, ready to swing the section of a tent pole he'd found.

Charlie watched the demonic shadows as the dismal carnage unfolded before him. He felt the fear race through him, taking hold of his body and paralyzing him and then he focused his energy on trying to breathe. It was all too unreal for him. This wasn't supposed to happen. He thought about how insignificant his problems had been before now and how he had thought they were so important at the time. The lost relationship with his wife, Brianna and the depression he suffered when he lost his position at the bank he managed. There was a cold chill that sank into his bones as a drop of sweat rolled, as if in slow motion, down his forehead making it just to his cheek.

A shadow grew monstrous and ever closer to the wall and it wasn't until it crashed through door that Charlie was broken from his state of shock. To all of their surprise it was Anna. She had commandeered a vehicle in the confusion and drove it through the carnage right into the front of the giant tent. Waving in the window, she ordered them all into the Hummer and none of them failed to obey her. Within seconds they had piled in and she had torn her way out the other side, pieces of tent dragging behind them as the Hummer's engine roared.

Chapter Five

A spine cringing screech pierced through the armor of the Hummer. It made the occupants teeth clinch as a set of claws ran down the side of the vehicle. When the creature's final nail slipped from the rear quarter panel another Chupacabra leapt.

This one was more successful than its predecessor. Its claws sank deep into the roof, gleaming in the failing sunlight. It let out a gurgling roar, punching forward until it was able to peer over the edge and into the vehicle through the windshield.

Anna reached into her jacket and drew a pistol. She handed the gun to Adam as the creature hurled its claws into the window. The windshield split where the nails struck causing it to spider web as Adam fired the weapon through the roof. There was a loud roar followed by a thud as the Chupacabra rolled behind the Hummer, coming to rest in Anna's rear view mirror.

Everyone seemed to simply breathe for a while as they sped away. The only sound came from the humming of the wheels on the pavement. Brian was the first to break the silence. "Why do I get the feeling that you haven't told us everything?"

"Look," Anna said, "I could have left you back there, but I came and got you! You should just be happy that I saved your skin."

Adam looked at Brian and then at Anna. "So, have you told us everything?" he asked, watching her as her face turned red. She pushed a wisp of hair back that was in her eyes and let out a deep breath.

"This wasn't supposed to happen," she said as she pulled a pack Doublemint gum from her side pocket. She ripped the tab open, pulling a stick from it. "None of this was supposed to happen."

Anna chewed the piece and then passed the pack back to Charlie who was eye balling it like a steak dinner after a famine. He and Mark graciously accepted one and then returned the pack back to the front.

"What do you mean, this wasn't supposed to happen?" Brian questioned with a look a distress on his chiseled face.

"This was not suppose to happen to us; not here. We had an agreement."

"With who?" Adam asked growing even angrier.

"With the Russians," she admitted as she took another piece of gum from the pack and shoved it into her mouth.

"In the days of the Jabberwocky it was believed that these once alien creatures could be destroyed by cutting their heads off. This was only momentarily effective though, for a mortal wound only caused the creatures body to prepare for a reproductive metamorphous," she said chewing furiously on the gum.

"Once the metamorphosis was complete, the creature would take on a conical form splaying its needles out in an attempt to prick some unsuspecting animal. It was believed then that if pricked a poison would take hold of the animal, thus possessing it and eventually turning it into a Jabberwocky itself.

It was rumored for some time that one such creature had haunted a small village in Siberia. The people had little food to begin with and as the Jabberwocky slaughtered their cattle, they became desperate.

According to my sources, one night, in a heavy snow, twenty-four men set out to kill the Jabberwocky. They tracked it for miles until they realized it had lured them away, circled around them and then had gone back to the village," she continued, pushing the hair out of her face.

"When they returned to the village they found that most of the women and children had been killed. One woman rose up against it though. Helena Selimaj. Even though it had gashed her wide open she still managed to split it down the middle with a meat cleaver.

Apparently, some of the men rushed in, just as the creature fell dead. Its body curled and formed the cone as Helena fell into a coma. Later Helena would die from her wounds.

The men," Anna said, glaring over at Adam, "in their ignorance, believed it would be best to burn the cone and destroy any chance of it coming back. This would prove to be their undoing. Unknowingly, they sent the cone into the pyre and it is said that it burned as bright as a star. Many of the men stayed to see it burn until there were but flickering coals in the ashes. To their surprise though the cone remained and within a bat of their eyes the cone exploded sending thousands of needles into the unsuspecting watchers.

The poison took hold of them quickly and those who were not struck knew what they must do. They killed those who were infected and cast their bodies into the pit. One of the infected managed to escape though. He ran, changing as he went, until he finally collapsed high in the Siberian Mountains."

"Thanks for the history lesson," Brian said sarcastically, "but could you just get to the point?"

"The point is they found it. In the 1980's they found the missing creature frozen in the mountains. The team that found it took it to a lab. Russian scientists then used it to produce more of the creatures. It was believed that once they learned how to control these creatures they would become powerful weapons.

To test them, they were loaded onto the space shuttle and transported…"

"Whoa, whoa, whoa," Mark interrupted. "You're full of shit. I can't possibly believe that the U.S. allowed Russia to transport this killer mutant thing into space. Especially during the cold war when the *Iron Wall* was our sworn enemy."

Wind whistled through the hole in the roof as Anna bestowed the dark history on them. "It seems crazy I know Mark, but it's true. The U.S.S.R and the U.S.A were never really competing. It was all a ruse.

The ultimate goal of both sides was to create a Social Democracy fueled by capitalism. This New Order would then be made manifest all over the globe."

"You're so full of shit! I swear to God, you are so full of shit," Mark yelled.

"This is fucked," Brian added, shaking his head in disbelief as he packed a large chew into his mouth.

"It's true Anna said sternly and I don't care if you believe me. Those things were loaded onto the shuttle and they were transported to the space station. If ya'll don't believe me, just think about those you've lost and all the soldiers that were just killed and if you still don't believe me then try popping the bubble you're living in with your pinhead."

"Alright; everybody cool it," Charlie warned like a father at his last wits end on a family vacation to hell. "Just finish your damn story, Anna."

Anna glared at Mark in the rearview mirror and began talking again. "As I was saying before the creatures were then kept frozen aboard NASA's Skylab until their scheduled time for deployment. With precise timing they were jettisoned from the station, striking the atmosphere during an anticipated meteor shower. Operation "Falling Star" was the first of these deployments, which landed in Puerto Rico. This is how the creature acquired the name El Chupacabra.

The experiments were conducted to see if there could be a so-called alien form of population control. It seemed perfect, a faked alien invasion. No governments would be blamed for meteors hitting the planet that contained alien life forms. This would further concrete the fear of alien invasion and the idea of a one-world government, forged to better "protect" the people of our planet.

It was thought to be a full proof plan. They create a controllable enemy and use it to drive fear into the people of the world. This constant threat of attack would keep them in check. People are more readily susceptible to giving up their freedom in exchange for government protection."

Adam looked at the gun in his hand then back at Anna then pointed it at her. "Are you kidding me," he said with his eyebrows furrowing. "You knew about this all along and you never warned anyone?" His hand broke out in a sweat against the handle as the sun flared across the barrel.

Anna just kept driving and chewing as the wind whistled. Her eyes fixed on the road while she popped another piece of gum from the pack and stuck it in her mouth. "Are you going to shoot me?" she asked with a smirk, a wad of gum bulging in her cheek, "or do you want to know my part in all this?"

Chapter Six

Somewhere along M-53 the Hummer pulled off and rolled to a stop in the parking lot of a motel 6. The engine choked and popped as Anna turned the ignition key off. "So, ya gonna shoot me?" she said in a soft calm voice.

"Shoot her, shoot her, shoot her," the three in back were yelling.

Adam looked at the men then back at Anna. With a lot of question in his sigh he lowered the weapon and tucked it into the back of his pants. "No. I'm not going to shoot you. I just... Oh Jesus."

Before Adam could give warning the lethal creature was upon them. With a crash it sent its sickle like claws through the rear driver's side window. The hard, blade like claws found the soft tissue of Marks temple sending glass and blood into Brian and Charlie's face.

Brian, in a panic, pulled the handle to the door and rolled out of the Hummer. Charlie followed behind him as the Chupacabra took a second swing. Its razor sharp nails thrust, tearing the headrest from the driver's seat as Adam pulled Anna towards him.

Screaming, Anna pressed further and further towards Adam, trapping his arm behind his back as he scurried for his weapon. The Chupacabra, snorted, peering its long head into the vehicle. Its spines rose as its eyes glared into Adams. Three shots rang as a roar of pain pierced the air.

As Adam and Anna squirmed out of the vehicle the creature flailed around in pain. Its claws ravaged the seats as its arms swung unconsciously in a fit of rage and pain. One of the swings clipped Anna's calf as she made her way out the passenger side door.

Scooping her off the ground, Adam ran for the lobby of the Motel 6 holding Anna in his arms. Brian and Charlie had already found their way inside. Charlie held the door open as Adam ran in, twisting the door lock behind them. Anna was crying and biting her lip from the pain as Adam laid her down on a love seat just inside the lobby.

"They're everywhere," Brian yelled as he hopped over the front desk, immediately falling as he disappeared behind the counter. His right foot had landed on the tile floor, but his left foot had landed on the severed head of the receptionist. In shock, Brian shot up immediately fumbling with the phone beneath the desk.

"Oh, Chri...Christ. They're inside," Brian muttered, wiping his nose with the back of his hand. Staggering, he pressed the phone to his ear. There was no dial tone. He clicked the receiver several times then smashed the hand set on the desk. The round speaker piece rolled across the floor, coming to rest beside Charlie's foot.

Charlie looked down at the piece in despair. There was a strange calm that came over him, a certain sense of utter helplessness. As the despair progressed it seemed to tune out all of the chaos in the room. It was the kind of mental numbing that happens during times of extreme duress. The mind, fully aware of the inevitable outcome, floods itself with endorphins in preparation for the body's destruction.

Brian had floundered back over the desk and was screaming at Adam. "Doesn't anybody have a fucking cell? We just need a phone. We need a phone!"

"Shut up! Shut up!" Adam told him as Anna squeezed his hand and cried in agony. Shadows darted back and forth on the floor as the sun blazed through the windows.

A disturbingly unnatural smile cracked along Charlie's face as a tear welled in his eye. The shadows on the floor grew further provoking the tear to swell. All life in the room seemed perverted and meaningless. It was as if the four of them had entered a slow motion machine, a mechanism bent on filtering reality from the fiber of their existence.

Adam, still working to control the uncontrollable, was trying to calm Brian, trying to talk some sense into him, trying to give them all reassurance. Officer Adam Douglass, the highest scores in his recruit school, the recipient of several medals of Honor and bravery, always a servant to his fellow man. Despite his ignorance, it was a testament to humanities will to survive, to prevail against insufferable odds.

The shadows became one.

Anna, feverish, was gripping her leg. The wound, puss filled and bleeding, was causing her to slip in and out of consciousness. For a moment she had seen that horrible tooth ridden face in the entrance door window. Her mind went black again transporting her to that endless void where even thought was dark and irrelevant.

Her head dipped and the light was back, fuzzy and painful. Delirious and reeling, she dismissed the images she kept seeing. She had seen her mother, vivid and beautiful, standing before her. Though her mother had passed some years ago, she had believed her to be real, but the darkness took her mother again and replaced her with that grizzly face.

She faded once more and when she came back the windows were filled with the terrible images of the Chupacabras. All of them peered at her dark and hungry. All of them fixated with their teeth gleaming, staring at Anna with their black and soulless eyes.

There was a terrible crash inside the motel 6; a deafening burst of breaking glass all around them, then the heavy nails clicking on the red porcelain tiles.

A tear ran down Charlie's face, staining his cheek as it went, breaking at his chin then falling into the shadow that consumed the light.

As the creatures flooded into the lobby the sounds of screams resonated then were replaced by the sounds of tearing flesh, shattering bones and the howling cries of the new dominant specie.

J L Carey Jr. is a writer and an artist living in Michigan with his wife and three children. He is an Instructor of English and Art and holds an MFA in Creative Writing from National University and a BA in English from the University of Michigan with a concentration in writing. He is currently a journalist at East Village Magazine and has had various stories and poems published in both print and online journals.

Other books by J L Carey Jr:
Turning Pages, poems 2010
Callous, In Spring Selected Poems 2013
Repressions Poems 2015
Songs of Epigenesis Poems 2016
The Reflection of Elias Dumont Novel 2016